Mayhem and the Mysterious Stranger

Mayhem Pet Detective Book Two

by

Melissa Behrend

Mayhem for Hire. Pet Detective.

Yes, he's an actual pet.

He's a hardboiled, hardheaded,

hardhearted Pointer, pointing in the direction

of truth.

Chapter One

"Good morning, Mayhem," Lucy said when Mayhem walked in the door of his office.

'Mayhem: Pet Detective' read the words on the sign out front.

Lucy was Mayhem's devoted assistant—a Basset Hound with a heart of gold.

"Morning, Lucy. Any new cases?" He stopped at her desk on his way to his office. Lucy's desk was neat and tidy. Mayhem's, on the other hand, not so much. He never remembered to file anything. Files, folders, and notes were piled everywhere.

"Yes, sir," she said, and handed him several pieces of paper—papers he would add to the mountain on his desk. They were phone messages from dogs who'd called in over the weekend asking for his help.

He grabbed the messages, walked into his office, and tossed his briefcase on his desk—sending papers, pens, and one shoe flying (Mayhem's owner had been looking for that shoe!). As he read through the messages, he shook his head. "No," he said and tossed the slip onto his desk. "Nope." He scrunched this one up into a ball and threw it toward the wastebasket. Two points! He got ready to throw the last one down and then stopped. "Wait a second…"

Mayhem walked back out of his office and stopped at Lucy's desk again. "This is interesting," he said, and showed her the message.

"Ah, yes," she nodded. "Lots of thefts in the neighborhood. Sounded like a good one to me, too."

"Who's this client? Chaos? Do we know him?" Mayhem asked.

Lucy shrugged. "I don't think so. But with your names, you guys should team up! Mayhem and Chaos, solving crimes all over the city!" She barked a laugh, but Mayhem didn't join in.

"Chaos and Mayhem," he mumbled, heading back to his office. "Sounds ridiculous. No one would hire us." Once he got back to his desk, he realized he'd forgotten to ask Lucy to call the client. "BARK! Lucy, please get Chaos on the phone. I want to hear more about these thefts. Might have a burglary ring on our paws."

Chapter Two

You see, Mayhem was a detective. A dog detective, sure, but a doggone good one. Like it said on his cards, "Mayhem for Hire". He was available for any kind of case—except the really boring ones.

Mayhem was a hardboiled, hardheaded, hardhearted detective. He was a Pointer, and he pointed in the direction of truth. He could sniff out the bad guy a mile away. Give him a scent, and he'd be on it. He'd track it to the ends of the earth if he had to. Mayhem could find your missing baseball mitt, the guy who stole your lunch money, or the one that got away. Just give him a call. He's Mayhem for Hire. And his rates are reasonable.

Chapter Three

"He's here, boss," Lucy said into the intercom.

"Send him in, please," Mayhem told her. He stood to meet Chaos, holding out a paw. A large black Labrador Retriever walked in and held out his paw, too. They shook, leaned forward and sniffed each other, and then they nodded.

"Yep. I thought I knew your scent. We go to the same groomer," Chaos said. At the word 'groomer' both dogs shuddered.

"Ugh, the groomer! She's very nice, but…" Mayhem said.

"Yeah. But who likes going to the groomer? Not me!" Chaos agreed, shaking his head like he had water in his ears.

"Sit," Mayhem said, "please." And Chaos did, sitting down in the only empty chair in the office. Not only was Mayhem's desk piled high with files, folders, and papers, but so was the floor, the bookshelves, and one of the chairs in front of his desk. The other, luckily, he kept clear for clients. Like Chaos. Mayhem handed him a treat and ate one himself. "So, these thefts? Where've they been occurring? Tell me everything you know."

"Well, my human takes me for a walk early in the morning, when it's still dark out—"

"Ah, bummer," Mayhem interrupted. "Early morning walks are the worst."

"You betcha," Chaos nodded. "I need my beauty sleep. But anyway, one morning, not so long ago, my human and I were out and we heard loud barking from the dogs down the street. Way louder than they shoulda been barking at that hour—unless something was wrong."

"So what was it? What were they barking at?" Mayhem asked, his head tilted to the left.

"Well, I stopped, trying to figure out what was wrong, but my human wanted to get a move on." Chaos sighed. "He had to get to work."

Mayhem shook his head. He knew those kinds of humans. "Did you ever figure out what were they barking at?"

"I did. Later that day, on my evening walk, we ran into Bert and Ernie, the two French Bulldogs from down the street. They told me bacon had been stolen right off their front porch!"

"Bacon! From their front porch?" Mayhem's eyes were bugging out of his head, and he was drooling a little. "Tell me more."

"Well, you know the local milkman? He delivers food, too. Our neighbors get a food delivery once a week, and someone must've known about it. Because they stole the bacon from the delivery box after it was delivered!"

"Wow. I don't know. I love bacon. I might be tempted to steal it, too." Mayhem said. Then he added, "But I would never."

Chaos barked out a laugh. "Right? Very tempting."

"So, you didn't get a look at the culprit?"

"No, sorry to say, he had already taken off. Nowhere to be found." Chaos's head perked up and he raised a paw. "But I did catch his scent."

"What was it like?" Mayhem asked. "And you said 'he'? You're sure our thief was male?"

"Yes. Definitely male. And the scent was wild. Feral. Nothing I'd ever smelled around there before."

"So maybe a stray?" Mayhem scratched his head.

"Maybe," Chaos said. "Or a runaway. Either way, doesn't give him an excuse to steal."

Chapter Four

"No, you're right. There's no excuse for stealing. Now, what else has gone missing? Besides the bacon?" Mayhem asked, notepad and pen at the ready.

Chaos sat forward in his chair. "Well, for starters, the poodle over on Avondale? Henrietta? She had one of those little balls with the bell inside?" Mayhem nodded. He knew the toy. "It was stolen a couple of weeks ago. At first, we all thought it had rolled away somewhere, but then once other dogs' toys started going missing, we decided maybe someone had taken it."

"Hmmm. Bacon and toys…" Mayhem stopped writing. "What else has been taken?"

"Let's see. I know the Corgi over by the park, Buster, his tug of rope toy is missing. And you know those things, you can't let 'em go. So if it's gone, it was stolen."

Mayhem nodded. He knew those ropes. "Why would this dog be stealing toys? And bacon?" Neither dog had an answer. "Once I solve this case, I'll ask him."

Mayhem stood up and headed out of the

office, motioning for Chaos to follow.

Chapter Five

"Hello, my name is Mayhem, and you already know Chaos," Mayhem said, holding out a paw to Henrietta, the poodle. She was sitting on the porch, behind a gate. Henrietta lived in a big house, with a huge front porch.

She laughed as she shook his paw. "Mayhem and Chaos! Are you guys a dog band? Do you sing?"

"NO," Chaos said, loudly. He did not like singing. Or music. He howled when his humans played it.

"Oh. Are you performers? Maybe actors? Do you travel around? Do you have an act?" she asked.

Mayhem shook his head in frustration. "No, no, no! I'm a private investigator, and Chaos is my client. He told me your toy was stolen? We're trying to figure out who is stealing from the dogs in this neighborhood."

"Oh," she said, disappointed. She titled her head. "Why didn't you say so?"

Mayhem let out a sigh. He'd been trying to say so! Mayhem studied the poodle in front of him.

She was tall, thin, and had very curly white hair.

Henrietta also wore a bow in her hair and had a

collar with lots of shiny things on it.

"Oh, good!" she said. "What can I do to help?" She sat back on her haunches to listen.

"Well, do you remember when you last had your toy?" he asked her, trying to nail down a time the mysterious stranger might have been in her yard.

"I think it was last week, on well, one of the middle days, because my human had just left for work. I was alone, and I like to amuse myself by smacking the ball under the coffee table and retrieving it."

"The coffee table? But that's inside…" Mayhem said, confused about how someone could steal if from inside her home.

"Right. But then I heard something outside, so I ran out back, through the doggy door, and I took my ball with me. So I wouldn't be too scared of whatever was outside."

"Ah, so it's your safety toy."

"Exactly," she said. "It was still a little dark out, and I needed it. I still do. So if you find it, please bring it back."

"We will. When you ran out back, what did you see? You said you heard a noise?"

"Oh, right! Yes! Well, I got distracted by a squirrel—" she said.

"So the noise was a squirrel?" Chaos asked.

"No, I don't think so—it sounded much louder than a squirrel. When I got outside, I didn't see anything out there," she said. Mayhem sighed. "At least not at first." Mayhem perked up again.

"What'd ya see?" he asked.

"Well, I heard another noise, this time off to the side, by the patio. I barked and turned to look, and I saw a dog running through our back yard. He jumped over our fence and took off."

"Did you get a good look at the culprit?" Mayhem asked. This was the lead he was looking for!

"Sort of. He was thin, wiry, and his fur sort of…flowed?"

"Like an Afghan Hound?" Mayhem asked, his head tilted, inquisitive.

"No, not like that at all. His hair wasn't as long as an Afghan's. I guess sort of a medium-haired dog?"

"Hmmmm," Mayhem said. "A medium-haired, thin, wiry dog who loves bacon. Not a lot to go on."

"Maybe we should talk to Buster next?" Chaos suggested.

"Let's go," Mayhem said.

"Oh, can I come?" Henrietta asked. "I want to find the dog who stole my ball!"

"Come on," Mayhem said. "The more the merrier."

And so the three of them high-tailed it to the park (and yes, their tails were high in the air).

Chapter Six

Mayhem, Chaos, and Henrietta approached the fence at the back of a blue and white house. They could hear a dog barking.

"Hello?" Mayhem called. They heard a 'yip' in return.

"Hi there!" Buster called. "Come on in!"

The three dogs looked around. "Um," Chaos said, "how?"

"Oh, right here!" The gate in front of them opened.

"How'd you do that?" Henrietta asked Buster as the three dogs filed into the backyard. The gate closed behind them.

"Lots of practice," he said. "Look!" He ran over to the closed gate, and they watched as he hopped up on his back legs and pulled on the handle. "Easy peasy!" The door swung open.

"Amazing. I need to learn how to do that," Henrietta said.

"Buster," Chaos said, "these are my friends Mayhem and Henrietta." The dogs all sniffed one another to say hello. "We're here to ask you some questions about the toy you lost. Mayhem's a detective. He's trying to figure out who the thief is."

"And get back our stuff!" Henrietta said.

"Oh, yay!" Buster said. "I want my rope back."

"What can you tell me about that day? The last day you remember having your rope?" Mayhem asked.

Buster sat down on his Corgi bottom and thought about it. He tilted his head to the side, and then he sniffed the air. Finally, he said, "Oh, I know! I was chasing a rabbit. I left the rope behind to try and get the bunny…and when I came back, it was gone. I thought maybe my human had it, but nope. I kind of forgot about it, to tell you the truth, until Chaos asked about missing toys."

Mayhem gave Chaos a funny look, as if he thought maybe the Lab had something to do with the thefts. Chaos shook his head, his paws up. "I asked around, trying to find out who else was missing something."

Mayhem thought about it a second. "But wait. You called me because things had gone missing around the neighborhood. Toys, food…but why would *you* call me? You didn't lose anything."

Chaos looked embarrassed. "Well, I—"

Henrietta barked. "Out with it, buddy."

"Okay, I did lose something. It's just…" Chaos said, his tail wagging nervously.

"Yes?" Mayhem asked.

"It's embarrassing! Whoever the thief is…he stole my stuffed bear." Chaos looked at the others, waiting to see if they'd laugh at him. No one did.

"Oh, I'm so sorry!" Henrietta said. "I know what it's like to have your safety toy taken from you. It's horrible!"

Buster nodded. "My rope's my favorite toy, too. I really miss it."

"Hmmm," Mayhem said, scratching his chin. "Looks like whoever's doing this is taking dogs' favorite things. And bacon. Which is everyone's favorite thing." The others nodded. Mayhem was smart.

"So what now? How do we find this guy?" Chaos asked. Mayhem had an idea.

"A stakeout! We'll set a trap for this guy, then sit back and watch. Works every time."

Chapter Seven

"Well, maybe not every time," Mayhem said, disappointed. The four dogs were up early, watching a spot in the park. They'd placed a squeaky stuffed squirrel in the middle of a green space, then hidden in the nearby bushes to watch.

Henrietta yawned. "I'm so tired. I don't think anyone's coming."

"Oh, wait! Look!" Buster said.

Mayhem pointed. "Someone's coming!"

They all got quiet and stared at the shape coming toward them. As it got closer, they all sighed. "Ah, man," Chaos said, sniffing the air. "She's not the thief! She's only a little human."

"But look! She took the stuffed squirrel," Henrietta said as the little girl picked up the toy. "Are you sure she isn't the thief?"

Chaos shook his head. "Nope. Wrong smell."

"And look," Mayhem said, pointing again, "she's looking around for the owner of the toy!"

"Uh oh," Buster said, "we've been spotted!" But instead of running away, Buster jumped up and ran to the little girl. He barked and hopped at her feet, licking her hand when she offered it to him. Then she gave him the stuffed squirrel. Buster grabbed it and brought it back over to the group.

"She's the nicest human," Buster said. "Look! She gave me the squirrel."

"So she's not the thief," Mayhem said. "Unless, of course, she's stealing our toys and giving them to other dogs." Then he barked out a laugh. "But I don't think so."

"Besides, she's got the wrong smell," Chaos said again, shaking his head.

"Now what?" Buster asked.

"More detecting," Mayhem said.

Chapter Eight

"What are we doing here?" Henrietta asked. It was the next day, and all the dogs had gathered in Mayhem's office. Once they got there, he'd told them they were going on a field trip and led them here.

"I've never even seen this place before. What is it?" Buster asked, staring up at the gray building. The building was two stories, with lots of windows. All the windows had blinds that were halfway down, so they looked like sleepy eyes. But it wasn't a sad building; every one of those windows had fun, colorful pictures in it—bees, rainbows, unicorns, stars, even dogs and cats.

"This is—" Mayhem said, but was cut off as the doors in front of them flew open and little kids came running out every which way.

"A daycare!" Chaos shouted. The kids spotted them and started to 'ooh' and 'aah' over them.

"Puppies!" one little boy shouted.

Buster barked, but Henrietta was upset. "I'm no puppy!" she said. "I'm grown."

"Ah, Henri, let 'em call you a puppy. To kids, we're all puppies," Buster said, laughing. He was right. Kids thought all dogs were puppies. Mayhem didn't mind. He just wanted to get some information out of the dog who worked there.

"Come on," he said, and led them inside. The children noticed, but the older humans were too busy corralling the kids to pay the dogs any attention. The four dogs slipped down the main hallway to the door marked 'Administration Office'.

"This is the place," Mayhem said, pushing the door open with his nose. "Hey, Waffles," he whispered to a Boxer who was all curled up on a blanket next to her owner's desk. The dog looked up. First her lip turned up in a growl, upset at being awakened, but then she smiled.

"Hey! Mayhem!" she said, getting up and coming over to sniff everyone. "Are you here about my bed?"

"You guessed it," Mayhem said.

"Her bed?" Chaos asked. "I thought we were here on my case."

"We are," Mayhem said. "I'm pretty sure your cases are the same. Waffles reported her bed stolen about a week ago, and I've been looking for it ever since. So far, no leads. Until you showed up, Chaos."

Both dogs looked at him and tilted their heads. "Did your bed get stolen, too?" Waffles asked, looking at Chaos.

Chaos shook his head. "No, but stuffed bear was stolen and so was my neighbor's bacon—"

"And our toys were stolen," Henrietta said, interrupting.

Waffles looked surprised. "Bacon? And toys? Who is doing this? And why?"

"That's what I'm going to find out," Mayhem said. "I'd like to ask you a couple of questions about the morning you found your bed gone."

Waffles nodded. "Sure, anything."

"You told me before," he said, "you came into work with your human and when you went to take your mid-morning nap, it was gone."

"Yep. We took a walk before work, I had breakfast, and then when I got here, I was exhausted. I needed to take a nap to recharge before the kids arrived. When I walked over to my bed, though, it was gone! I had to sleep on the floor."

"What happened when you alerted your human?" Mayhem asked.

"She was clueless. I barked and she came running. We searched everywhere. She opened doors, looked in cabinets, but nothing. My bed was gone," Waffles said.

"And you didn't see anyone strange when you came in that morning? Smell any unfamiliar scents? Find anything odd, maybe left behind by the thief?" Mayhem asked.

Waffles sat down to think. She tilted her head one way, then she tilted it the other. She scratched behind her ear. Then she stood up. "OH! Yes! I remembered something! When we came in that morning, there was an odd scent in the air. Sort of…wild? I remember I started to follow the scent down the hall but my human told me to come back, and I did. Not sure if the scent was the thief's or not, but there *was* some gray fur near the window in our office."

"Can you show us where?" Mayhem asked.

"Sure, right this way." The dogs followed Waffles over to one of the windows. The window was so low they could all see out of it, and her new bed was right below it.

"So this is probably where he got in. And out," Chaos said, and everyone nodded. Made sense to them.

"Hmm," Mayhem said. "Gray fur. Wild scent. Stealing toys, beds, and food. Who is this mysterious stranger?"

Chapter Nine

"Thanks for meeting me," Mayhem whispered. Chaos sat beside him. The streetlights were on, but the sun was coming up. Chaos had already gone for his morning walk with his human. Once his human left for work, Chaos slipped out to meet Mayhem. Now they sat side by side on a small hill next to Chaos's house, watching the street.

"Do you think we'll see him?" Chaos asked.

Mayhem shook his head. "Who knows. But we know he stole food from your neighbors a few weeks ago. If he's hungry, he may try again. It's a long shot, but until we catch his scent again, this is all we have."

Chaos nodded. Then he gasped. "LOOK!" Mayhem did. The mysterious stranger was sneaking up the street toward them, walking lightly on his padded paws. The animal crept up to the neighbor's porch and pushed open their delivery box. He rooted around inside, then slipped something out.

"Looks like…" Chaos said.

"A carton of eggs?" Mayhem said, surprised. "That'll be hard to run with!"

Then he and Chaos jumped up, barking. The animal spun around, saw them, and took off. Chaos and Mayhem gave chase! They followed the stranger up the street, around the corner, down the hill, but by the time they'd flown around the last corner, the dog was gone. Poof! Disappeared.

"Where'd he go?" Chaos asked. Mayhem was too busy following his nose to answer. Mayhem zoomed up the street, down the street, back the way they came, and then back toward Chaos again.

"I don't know? His scent seems to go in a circle. How's that possible?" Mayhem shook his head, scratched his chin, then his ears perked up. "OH! I know! Follow me!" Mayhem raced into the yard of the closest house, then ran to the fence. "Ah ha!" He pointed. There was a gap in the boards. He and Chaos sniffed, long and deep. "Yes!" Mayhem shouted. "It's him!"

"Well, what do we do now?" Chaos asked.

"Go through the fence, of course." Mayhem looked at Chaos like he was silly. "Watch!" Mayhem crouched down, got his snout through the opening and pushed. Next thing you know, he was through the fence! From the other side, he called, "Come on!"

And Chaos did. He used his strong Labrador muscles to muscle right through the opening, and then he raced behind Mayhem as they chased the scent once again.

"Now where'd he go?" Chaos asked, when they finally stopped running. The two dogs had run through backyards, dashed through fence gates, zoomed around bushes, and now they were standing in one of the neighborhood parks. In front of them? The woods.

"He must've gone into the woods," Mayhem said. "Which explains the wild, feral smell. He must live in there."

"Wow," Chaos said, "he must be brave. I wouldn't want to live in the wild." He shivered at the thought. Then they heard it. A howl. A yip. A yip-howl.

"I'm not sure he's a dog," Mayhem said, his eyes wide.

"No," Chaos said, shaking his head.

They looked at each other. At the same time they said, "He's a coyote!" They'd solved part of the mystery. Their mysterious stranger was a wild animal! A coyote.

"Explains why he needs to steal food, but why the toys?" Chaos asked.

"Let's find out," Mayhem said.

"You mean…?"

"Yep! Follow the howls!" Once again, they ran. They ran through the trees, jumping over small creeks, scrabbling over rocks, and busting through the brush until they came upon a den.

Mayhem stopped and pointed. Chaos looked. "A den! This must be where he lives!"

"Right," Mayhem said, "and where there's a coyote den…" A little head popped out of the den. "There are cubs." A second tiny head popped out of the den. And then another. And another!

"Look at all the babies," Chaos whispered.

"Uh oh," Mayhem said as a much larger head popped out. He backed up and ran right into Chaos. The cubs' mom stared right at them—and then she growled. Mayhem raised a paw. "We're not here to hurt you—or to get hurt."

"No," Chaos said, "we're just here to…"

"What?" a deep voice asked. The mysterious stranger they'd been chasing was the cubs' dad, and he didn't look very happy to see them.

"We're here to get back our friends' toys," Mayhem said. "We think you took them." One of the cubs giggled and came out of the den with a rope toy in his mouth. Buster's rope toy. And

then another cub came out, pushing Henri's ball.

Mayhem and Chaos looked at each other and shrugged. "But it looks like you guys probably need them more than our friends do," Chaos said. "Or I do," he added as a third cub came out carrying Chaos's stuffed bear.

"Look, I'm sorry for stealing their things," the coyote said, "but there aren't a lot of places out here to find toys for your kids."

"Or bacon?" Mayhem asked. They all laughed.

"Or bacon," the coyote said. "They're hungry. I have to do what I can to feed them. By the way, my name's Sebastian. And this is my wife Bella."

Bella smiled and nodded at them. "We do our best to find food. Sometimes that means taking whatever we can find."

Mayhem nodded. He understood. He'd never lived in the woods, on his own, but he'd heard the stories. "Hey," he said, "I have an idea. I think we

can help."

Chapter Ten

"Here's another one, Mayhem," Lucy said, handing him a stuffed giraffe.

"Thanks, Lucy! Who brought this one?" he asked as he put it into the box.

"Bert. Or Ernie. I get those two confused," she said with a shrug.

"Lucy, they were nametags. And different sweaters," he told her.

"Oh, I know, but I always forget who's who.'

Chaos laughed as he brought over some bully sticks. "I'm donating these. I love them, but I know the cubs will, too."

"Ah," Henrietta said, "that's so nice of you." She had selflessly allowed the cubs to keep her ball and had even brought in an old bed. "I've got beds all over the house," she told them. "I'll never miss this one. Plus, I know it'll keep the cubs warm at night—and that makes me happy."

Buster had also allowed the cubs to keep his tug of war rope and added another rope toy to the mix. When Mayhem told everyone his idea to collect food, toys, and bedding for the coyote family, they all pitched in. Dogs they didn't even know heard about it and brought in treats, toys, and blankets. Donations poured in for days.

"Alright, guys, I think this is good. Let's head to the park and give the Sebastian and Bella a surprise!" Mayhem said. This time, the dogs took a more direct route to the park, instead of racing through backyards and crawling under fences.

Once they got to the coyotes' den, four little heads popped out again. "Oh, my goodness!" Henri said. "Aren't you guys the cutest?"

"Hello!" Sebastian said, popping out after his cubs. "What do you have there?" He nodded to the bags the dogs held in their mouths.

"We brought snacks!" Chaos said.

"And warm bedding," Mayhem said.

"And toys!" Buster said. The cubs swarmed Buster, trying to get a look at those toys.

Their parents laughed. "Down, kids! Take it easy!" Everyone laughed as the cubs grabbed toys and ran back to their den.

"Mayhem, we can't thank you enough for all you've done. Thank you all!" Bella said.

"Of course. It's the least we could do for the mysterious stranger in our neighborhood," Mayhem said. Then he looked at Chaos. "I believe we can say this case is closed?"

"I think so," Chaos said.

"You know," Mayhem said, "we work pretty well together. In fact, Lucy thought our detective agency could use a partner…"

"Chaos and Mayhem Investigations?" Buster asked. "Sounds great!"

"Well," Mayhem said, "I was thinking Mayhem and Chaos Investigations...but yeah. Whaddya say?"

Chaos barked. "I say, what's our next case, partner?"

Woof! Woof! (The End)